RETURNS	Items must be returned or renewed on or before closing time on the last date marked above
RENEWALS	Unless required by other members, items may be renewed at the loaning library in person, or by post or telephone, on two occasions only.
INFORMATION NEEDED:	Member's card number.
MEMBERSHIP	Please notify any change of name or address.
STOCK CARE	Please look after this item. You may be charged for any damage.

JIM DOWNER   TED HUGHES

Timmy the Tug

Timmy was a paddle-boat, sound as a gong,
  Not a worm in his timbers, fresh paint all over.
He was hale as a whale and twice as strong,
  And he sailed on the peaceful river.

Now Timmy had paddles, you can all see that,
  But propellors are now in fashion
  And ships that charge through ocean,
So the captain quit with the cook and the cat
  And a whole six months rum ration.

And found a ship that sailed high seas,
  With mighty propellors and huge freights,
And he left Timmy for the gulls to tease,
Moored with rough ropes to the sleepy Quays,
  While rust ate the paint off his plates.

2600

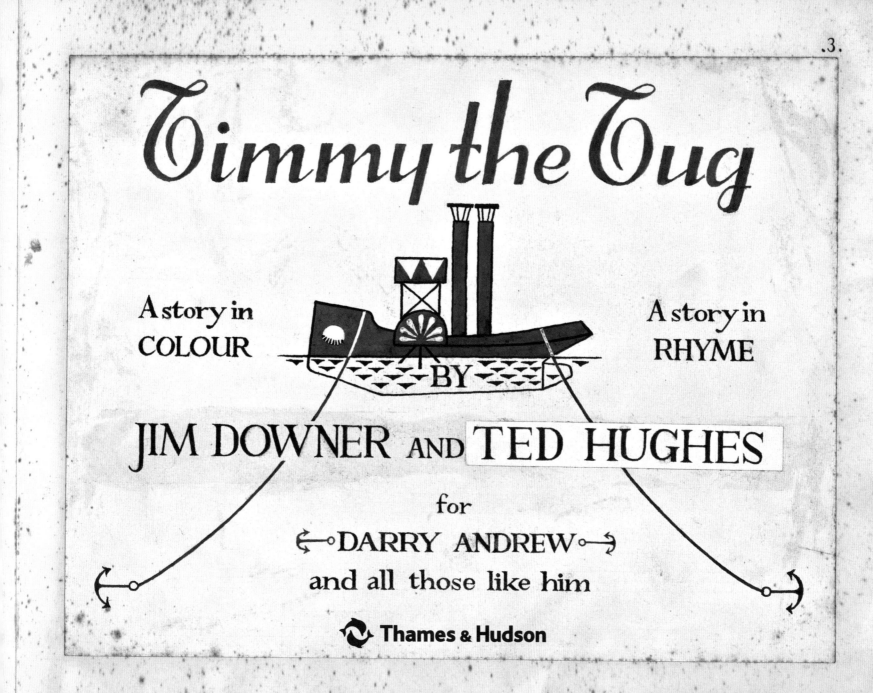

Timmy the Tug

A story in
COLOUR

A story in
RHYME

BY

JIM DOWNER AND TED HUGHES

for
↤ DARRY ANDREW ↦
and all those like him

Thames & Hudson

Timmy the Tug sat patiently there.
  The ropes rubbed sore, his rivets ached.
he was up to his eyes in oil and tar.
The gulls cried 'Old Crock' in his ear,
  The green crabs called him wrecked.

This was more than he could stand.
  He closed his eyes, he counted ten:
"I'd be far better off as a house on land,
Or a triangle in a bad brass band,
  At least I'd be useful then."

Like a weight-lifter Timmy then
  Took one tremendous breath,
Drew the ropes till he felt the strain,
And then heaved with the strength of ten,
  While the harbour churned beneath.

He would escape! At his fierce look
  The gulls hid in a cloud,
The quays trembled, the harbour shook.
He would escape! Or he would pluck
  The quays from where they stood.

Then with cracks like the shots of a gun
  The ropes snapped suddenly.
His paddles whirl, - the last rope's gone, -
The tall cranes dance to see it done, -
  Timmy the Tug is free.

Now fast he chugs and he chugs far.
  As far as he can see
The blue sky and the blue sea are.
He chugs along without a care,
  Until, suddenly,

Almost too late, he stops, - he sees
  Almost on top of him
Two great tugs made to sail the seas
(Tim scarcely comes up to their knees)
  And they pull after them

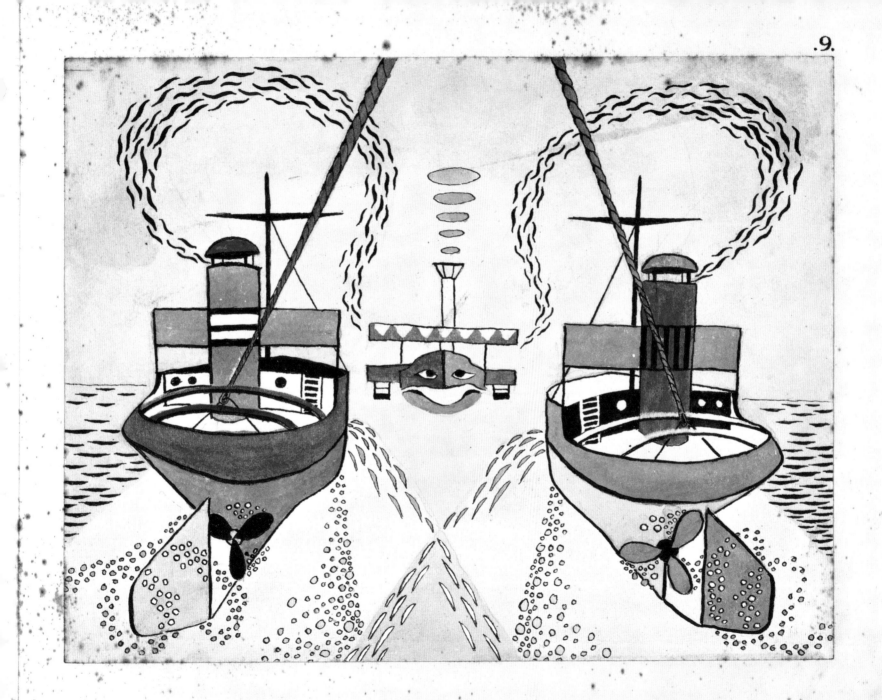

A huge liner, a castle, with towers,
  So high it covers the sun.
Each tug straight ahead stares,
Neither sees Timmy, neither cares,
  And the huge liner comes on.

Timmy dives left, and he dives right,
  He dives up, he dives down,
He paddles round with all his might -
No corner ever was so tight -
  Then those great ships have gone.

"A piece of clever paddling, that."
    Timmy said with pride.
"I did not even lose my hat.
A cat's not easier on its mat
    Than I on the ocean-tide."

He romps up to a trawler then.
    Its nets spread through the sea
With swarms of fishes struggling in,
And every one waving a fin:
    "Set us free, set us free."

In dashes Timmy: "I know well "
  He cries, "What prison is."
Upon the meshes then he fell,
The tangle he made was terrible,
  And out jumped every fish.

Timm y's tangled paddles stopped.
  The angry trawler came:
"Be off, or else you shall be chopped
In two, and both your funnels lopped."
  Tim almost sunk for shame.

And all around an angry crowd
  Of trawlers watched him go,
Blowing their foghorns long and loud
To teach him he was not allowed
  To treat his betters so.

The waves grew higher, the sea grew deeper,
　　But he never once looked back.
Till on a rock, green with sea-creeper,
He saw a stranded ship, and the skipper
　　Fired rockets from the wreck.

"Ahoy! Ahoy!" - he heard its cry.
　　He shouted back:"Avast!
You shall not long sit high and dry,
I'll set you sailing perfectly."
　　Here was his chance at last.

He piled on steam, and the foam flew
    As he cut through the sea.
This was the kind of work he knew,
To save a ship with all her crew,
    Not setting fishes free.

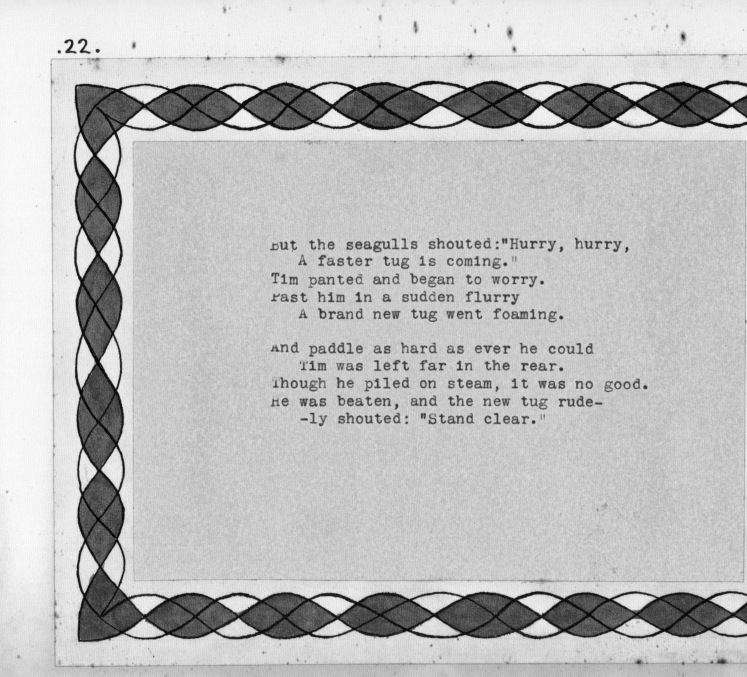

But the seagulls shouted:"Hurry, hurry,
   A faster tug is coming."
Tim panted and began to worry.
Past him in a sudden flurry
   A brand new tug went foaming.

And paddle as hard as ever he could
   Tim was left far in the rear.
Though he piled on steam, it was no good.
He was beaten, and the new tug rude-
   -ly shouted: "Stand clear."

Alas, Jimmy had lost his chance.
    He turned round in shame.
The new tug gave him a scornful glance,
And shouted again:"Be off at once
    Back the way you came."

Timmy sailed on, and on further,
    Into the dark North.
All the weather was foul weather,
Tumbling the geese and the clouds together
    For all it was worth.

The hail fell. There was no sun.
    Like a hammer the wind beat.
But Timmy sang as he sailed on:
"I'm more than a match for anyone
    Or anything I may meet."

Then he saw in full sail,
  And lovelier than a bird,
A ship on the sea's green racing hill.
Her sails were fine, her masts were frail,
  And through them the storm roared.

Timmy's eyes opened wide
  To see that lady go
Into the pits of sea, and ride
The cliffs of sea on the other side
  Making rodeo

Playfully of the bully gale.
  Then Timmy's heart jumped
As with crack and shriek her sail
Was torn off at a sudden squall:
  Down in the sea she slumped.

"I'm here, I'm here, never despair !"
   Cried Timmy, and he sped.
Waves rose like mountains everywhere,
But nothing there was that he would not dare.
   He puffed till his funnels went red.

"Oh save me, sir! Oh save me, sir!"
   "Or I shall surely drown.
My sails of costly taffeta,
My yard-arms fifty pounds a pair
   Into the sea go down."

Timmy reached her where she lay
   Weeping for her mast.
He acted then without delay,

Cast her a rope and hauled away
   Back to the harbour fast.

The light-house and the tall tall cranes
  Are the first to see him.
The low stone quay is taking pains
To stand on tiptoe, and strains its veins
  Wishing it could be him.

The seagulls cheer, the small waves bow,
  Curtsy and wave a hand.
High with pride is Timmy's prow
As home he leads his lady now
  The happiest tug in the land.

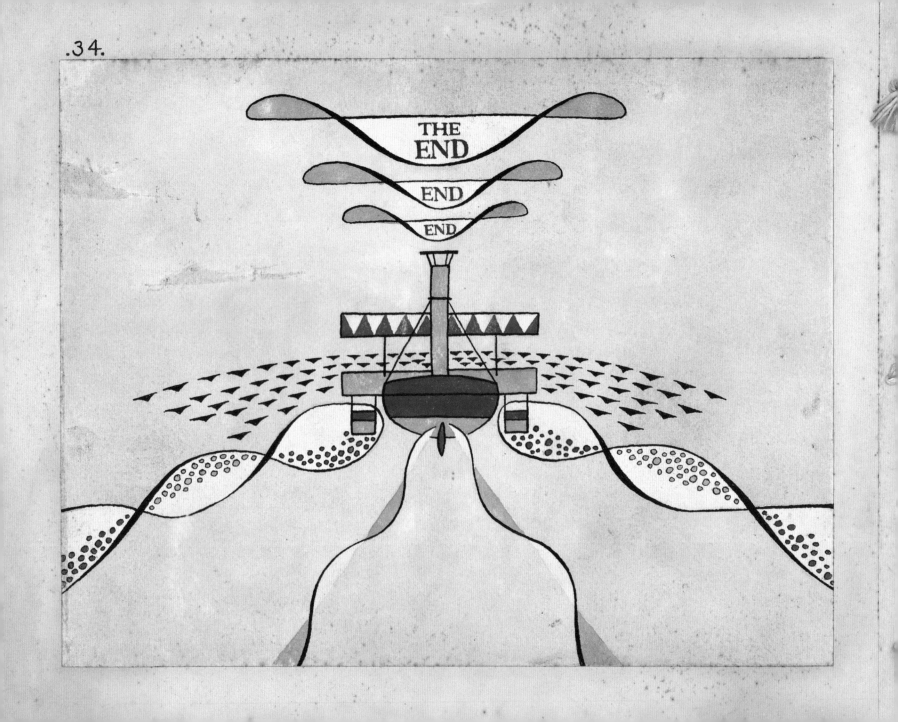

AFTERWORD

JIM DOWNER

This book was devised, illustrated and written over fifty years ago, between 1953 and 1956. The idea for it came to me while I was living in the top-floor flat of a Georgian terraced house in Bloomsbury, central London. At the time, I had just met Wendy, who was later to become my wife. Creating this book was all about impressing her that I was a suitable sort of husband — someone who might even make a good father, and someone who perhaps had the romantic ambition of being an artist.

At the time, art and design were very much 'in the air'. It was the period following the 1951 Festival of Britain, and the country was still full of a new sense of optimism and excitement that the festival had given us. Suddenly, anything and everything seemed possible. Colour had returned to a grey world, and we were all going to make the most of it.

From 1946 to 1951 I had studied painting at Leeds College of Art, after which I spent four months in Italy walking from Rome to Venice. On my return to England, finding that my paintings were not selling, I spent some further months walking through Yorkshire, repainting — and sometimes redesigning — pub signs, which had deteriorated during the war years. Although I received free board and lodging, the pay was not good, and I was forced to look around for a more settled job.

An opportunity came through the advice of Alan Taylor, one of my tutors at Leeds. He had a friend, Monty Reed, who was an exhibition designer looking for an assistant. This was perfect, for I had developed an interest in design and architecture while in Italy. As in England after the Festival of Britain, Italy was exploding with new visual and spatial thinking, which, during the time I was there, changed my ambitions from wanting to be a painter to wanting to be a designer. Moreover, the job was in London; where else should an ambitious designer be?

So, in the spring of 1952, I moved into the top-floor flat at 18 Rugby Street, Bloomsbury. The rent cost me my weekly wage (which was good for the time) plus £7. The main advantage, though, was being taught to be a professional designer by Monty Reed at his studio round the corner in Lamb's Conduit Street.

I was twenty-two, and the Rugby Street flat was the first home of my own. I could paint the walls any of the new colours, choose my own fittings, have exposed floorboards. In short, I could express what a fine designer I was, and, indeed, be a 'man about town' in what I then thought was the lap of luxury.

The house at 18 Rugby Street is early Georgian, four storeys high plus a basement. At that time, each floor was a separate flat, and each flat had its own tenant. All the flats had the same layout: you entered straight off the stairs into your living-room, which had two full-height windows looking out on to Rugby Street. To the right of the windows, over the staircase, was a boxed-off area that served as the kitchen. It had its own window — the third in the row of equally spaced windows viewed from the street. The kitchen was about six feet square, and contained a gas cooker that leaked so badly that you could never keep a houseplant longer than a few days. There was no bathroom; to have a bath you went to the nearby Holborn Public Baths. There was no lavatory either; the nearest was situated in the coal cellar, which was reached by going out of the front door,

turning left and going down steps behind railings to a space beneath the pavement. The lavatory itself, set to one side of a pyramid of coal, was always black with coal dust. There was no washbasin. At night, when your torch battery was in danger of fading or the Bloomsbury wind might blow out your candle, you had to be desperate to venture down.

There was no electricity in the house: both lighting and cooking were by gas. Each floor had its own gas meter, which took one-shilling coins. At night, every now and again you would be plunged into darkness as the meter ran out of its share of your income. I was paid on a Thursday evening, and during the winter regularly ran out of money on a Tuesday. Rather than sit in darkness with a candle, on Tuesday and Wednesday evenings I would go to Holborn Underground station and buy a twopenny ticket and go round and round London on the Circle line, enjoying the train's light and warmth while reading a good book.

Our lighting being by gas involved the use and continued replacement of gas mantles. They were small domes woven from fine-thread asbestos soaked in rare earth compounds. They were very delicate, and as you manipulated them into place often broke between the fingers, especially if you tried to do it in the dark or by the dim glow of a smoking candle. Heating was by coal fire, the coal for which had to be carried up from the space under the pavement. Sometimes, on a cold winter's evening, you had to wait in line to gain access to the coal cellar.

There was no supply of running water in any of the flats; water was obtained from a sink, with one cold-water tap, on the nearest half-landing between floors. So, one flight of stairs down for me; one flight of stairs up for the tenant on the floor below. That is how I came to meet Ted Hughes. His flat – which he used at odd times when up from Cambridge and elsewhere – was on the second floor, two below my own, but the sink just above his flat was blocked and he had just continued on up the stairs in search of water.

Even the sharing of a basin can lead to a friendship, and so it was in this case. We both had the advantage – or disadvantage – of having been brought up in Yorkshire; we both had the Yorkshireman's puritan work ethic; we had both spent teenage years walking the wild parts of the country. In addition, we both believed in the survival of the fittest. Rugby Street was the ideal place to exercise this attitude, and it drew into its space people of similar thinking. Without such a view, they did not stay long.

With no electricity, no television, and usually no money left to buy batteries for the wireless, we happily spent our evenings talking, often into the early hours, drinking instant coffee and, when we were flush, bottles of Bulls Blood. As a group, we often made suppers together, creating spaghetti bolognaise or macaroni cheese. I don't remember us ever venturing into vegetables.

We were a changing group of mostly twenty-year-olds living in and around Rugby Street, of various backgrounds and education but all determined to make the best of ourselves. There was Ted, and later, for a while, Sylvia Plath; there were the actors Peter O'Toole, Albert Finney and Siân Phillips, all then at RADA; there was the painter Robert O'Brian, living round the corner in Great Ormond Street; there were the potters Lucie Rie and Hans Coper; occasionally there was Jacques Tati, when he was in London, and Wendy Craft, whom I was busy courting. Wendy was Jacques's film editor and was then working on the English version of *Monsieur Hulot's Holiday*. Of course, we all called Jacques 'Hulot'. And there was Philip Wrestler, who was later to direct the Mini Cooper race around Turin in *The Italian Job*.

The talk was mostly about the arts. I remember how we all clubbed together to buy batteries for a radio so that we could listen to Richard Burton reading the first performance of *Under Milk Wood* on the BBC's Third Programme. I remember, too, Peter O'Toole singing the songs, word perfect, from *West Side Story*, having heard them earlier on a disc smuggled in from the USA, the record being unavailable in Britain at the time. There was also an evening when Ted and Sylvia kept a group of us enthralled by taking apart the anonymous ballad 'From the hag and hungry goblin' and then putting it together again, slightly differently, to our glee.

We did not see Sylvia very often, but there were times when Ted would read the poems that she and he were working on, inviting our observations. Indeed, we all put our work up for comments, and received them. Peter O'Toole gave us renderings of his lines for Sean O'Casey's *Juno and the Paycock*, which he was preparing at RADA. He spoke with a very good Irish accent, which was quite something, as, having also been brought up in Yorkshire, his everyday accent still had a slight touch of Alan Bennett about it. The stories Peter told us about his time at RADA would have us howling, and I was somehow inveigled into designing stage sets for them on a strictly no-fee basis.

Lucie Rie, with quiet excitement, would sometimes bring in a pot in order to show us a new colour in her glazes. The memory of the fragility of those colours on such slim vessels has been a permanent part of my visual awareness. So, too, has been the work of Richard Huws, who had the third-floor flat in Rugby Street. He had designed a 30-foot-high fountain of cascading water for the Festival of Britain, and it was still working on London's South Bank in the mid-1950s. The fountain caused enchanted excitement, and we all held Richard in awe.

For those of us in our twenties, a lot of the talk was about our futures. Would we 'make it'? Peter O'Toole seemed very sure he would, and, if he did have doubts, it never showed. In fact, his optimism was infectious, and when he was around he had us all soaring. The rest of us were perhaps less sure. We were certain that Britain was going forward with increasing speed, and we were all worried that we would be left behind. If only we were, say, a couple of years older and that much further ahead in our careers. Wendy, by contrast, already had her feet on the ladder, for, having started as an eighteen-year-old freelance film editor, she had already assisted Carol Reed and David Lean as well as Jacques Tati.

Before he met Sylvia Plath, Ted Hughes had put his name on the waiting-list for one of the £10 assisted-passage boat tickets to Australia, provided by the Australian government to attract those with 'get-up-and-go' to a new life away from a Britain that still had selected rationing. The scheme was popular, and Ted wished to join his brother Gerald, who had recently made the move. Ted also had thoughts of sailing his own boat to Australia, and as I had some experience of sailing, we spent evenings going over the possibilities. With no capital, however, even the cheap boats that had rotted over five years of war were not within reach, and they would have surely sunk before Land's End.

On different evenings, different mixes of people often talked on into the small hours, when, somnolent with gas fumes, we would venture into the early morning and walk into Covent Garden, or to Smithfield, to drink mugs of tea accompanied by an entire eighteen-inch fruit pie (usually cherry) in the all-night porters' cafés. At that time, Ted sported a black corduroy jacket of which Peter O'Toole and I were extremely covetous. We continually asked Ted where he had bought it, but he would never tell us. He wore it when he went off to St George the Martyr in Holborn to marry Sylvia. I later discovered that he had dyed it from a brown one. It was entirely right for his wedding.

Of course, not every evening was spent socially; in fact we were usually doing our own thing, looking after our own futures. I was drawing *Timmy the Tug*, trying to keep it hidden from Wendy whenever she called by. The pages were first drawn up in fine pencil; then watercolour was applied in washes. Finally, the pencil lines were gone over with Indian ink applied with a very fine mapping pen. This sequence of working was dictated by the fact that the ink was not waterproof, but you still had to be careful not to smudge it as you worked, for it took a while to dry. Sometimes this work was done in daylight at the weekend, but more often it was carried out under gaslight in the evenings.

Eventually *Timmy the Tug* was finished, including my rather amateurish verses. It was then that Ted, dropping in for a coffee, saw what I had done. Until then no one had seen it, for, as I have said, it was to be a surprise for Wendy. I did, though, want Ted's opinion. Ted, always generous, was kind about the verses, and then quietly asked if I would like him to provide his own version. Having no illusions about my writing, I accepted, and handed over the original illustrated manuscript, which he took away to work on in his flat.

The time had arrived when we were all leaving the magic of 18 Rugby Street – Ted with Sylvia to America, Peter to *The Long and the Short and the Tall*, *Lawrence of Arabia* and beyond, and Wendy and I to marry. I did not, after all, require the help of Timmy to persuade her. We all continued to meet well into the sixties, but somehow I did not get Timmy back from Ted. I was leading a busy life, and so was he. We had moved on into different worlds.

Fifty-two years later, in 2008, Ted's wife, Carol Hughes, found *Timmy the Tug* among Ted's archive, and, after searching me out, she kindly returned it to me. To my delight, I found that Ted had written his verses.

NOTE FROM THE AUTHOR:
Ted Hughes speaks about 18 Rugby Street in his poem of that name in *Birthday Letters*, a collection of his poetry first published in 1998.

First published in the United Kingdom in 2009 by Thames & Hudson Ltd,
181A High Holborn, London WC1V 7QX

thamesandhudson.com

Concept, Design and Text by Jim Downer © 2009 Jim Downer
Verses © 2009 The Estate of Ted Hughes

British Library Cataloguing-in-Publication Data
A catalogue record for this book is available from the British Library

ISBN 978-0-500-514962

Printed and bound in China by C&C Offset Printing Co. Ltd.